Jump, Frog, Jump!

by Robert Kalan

pictures by Byron Barton

Greenwillow Books, New York

For my brother Bill, with love
Text copyright © 1981 by Robert Kalan.
Illustrations copyright © 1981 by Byron Barton.
First published in 1981 by Greenwillow Books; reissued in 1995.
All rights reserved. Manufactured in China by South China Co. Ltd.
www.harperchildrens.com
First Edition 20 19 18 17 16 15 14 13 12
The Library of Congress cataloged an earlier version of this
title as follows: Kalan, Robert. Jump, frog, jump!
"Greenwillow Books."
Summary: A cumulative tale in which a frog tries to catch
a fly without getting caught itself.   [1. Stories in rhyme.]
I. Barton, Byron.   II. Title.   PZ8.3.K1246Ju   [E]   81-1401
ISBN 0-688-80271-0   AACR2
ISBN 0-688-84271-2 (lib. bdg.)
New edition: ISBN 0-688-13954-X
ISBN 0-688-09241-1 (pbk.)

This is the fly that climbed out of the water.

This is the frog that was under the fly
that climbed out of the water.

How did the frog catch the fly?

Jump, frog, jump!

This is the fish that swam after the frog

that was under the fly

that climbed out of the water.

How did the frog get away?

Jump, frog, jump!

This is the snake that dropped from a branch

and swallowed the fish

that swam after the frog

that was under the fly that climbed out of the water.

How did the frog get away?

Jump, frog, jump!

This is the turtle that slid into the pond

and ate the snake that dropped from a branch

and swallowed the fish

that swam after the frog

that was under the fly that climbed out of the water.

How did the frog get away?

Jump, frog, jump!

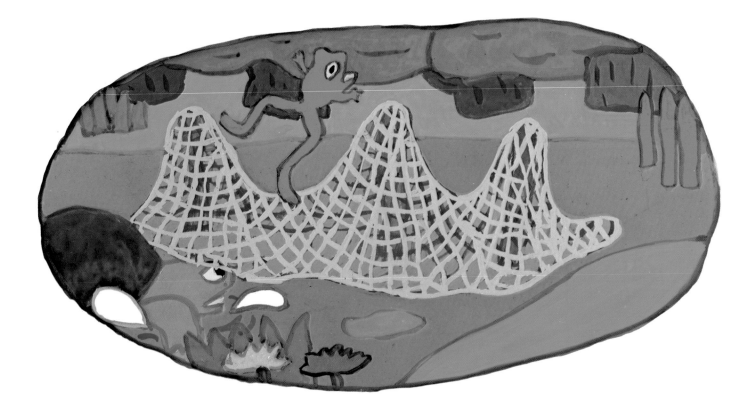

This is the net that wrapped around the turtle

that slid into the pond and ate the snake

that dropped from a branch

and swallowed the fish

that swam after the frog

that was under the fly that climbed out of the water.

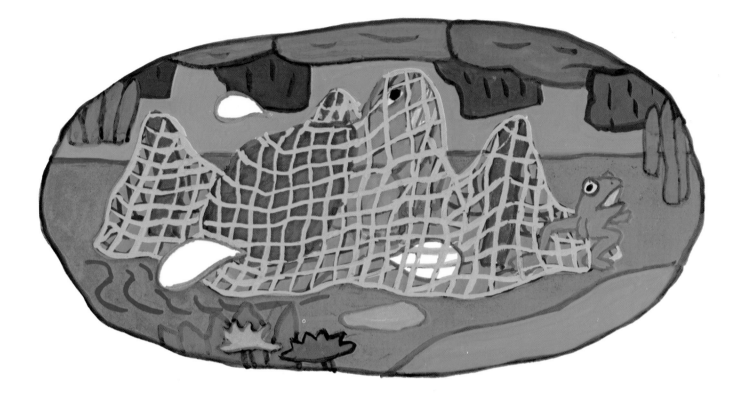

How did the frog get away?

Jump, frog, jump!

These are the kids who picked up the net

that wrapped around the turtle

that slid into the pond and ate the snake

that dropped from a branch

and swallowed the fish

that swam after the frog

that was under the fly that climbed out of the water.

How did the frog get away?

Jump, frog, jump!

This is the basket put over the frog

by the kids who picked up the net

that wrapped around the turtle

that slid into the pond and ate the snake

that dropped from a branch

and swallowed the fish

that swam after the frog

that was under the fly that climbed out of the water.

How did the frog get away?